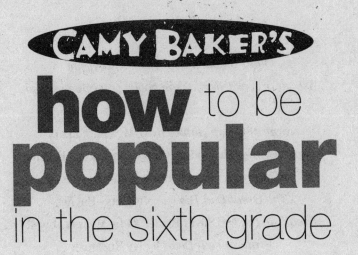

Camy Baker's

how to be
popular
in the sixth grade

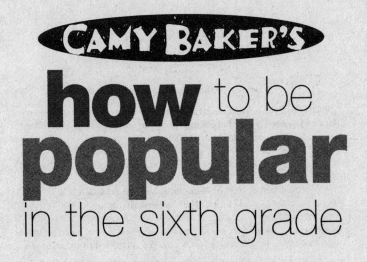

CAMY BAKER'S
how to be
popular
in the sixth grade

A SKYLARK BOOK

New York • Toronto • London • Sydney • Auckland

RL 5, 009–012

CAMY BAKER'S HOW TO BE POPULAR
IN THE SIXTH GRADE

A Bantam Skylark Book / September 1998

Skylark Books is a registered trademark of Bantam Books, a division of
Bantam Doubleday Dell Publishing Group, Inc. Registered in U.S. Patent
and Trademark Office and elsewhere.

A book by Memphis & Melrose Publishing Co.
All rights reserved.
Copyright © 1998 by Memphis & Melrose Publishing Co.
Cover art © 1998 by Bard Martin.

ISBN 0-553-48655-1

Published simultaneously in the United States and Canada.

Bantam Books are published by Bantam Books, a division of Bantam
Doubleday Dell Publishing Group, Inc. Its trademark, consisting of the
words "Bantam Books" and the portrayal of a rooster, is Registered in
U.S. Patent and Trademark Office and in other countries. Marca
Registrada. Bantam Books, 1540 Broadway, New York, New York 10036.

PRINTED IN THE UNITED STATES OF AMERICA

OPM   0   9   8   7   6   5   4   3   2   1

introducing
me

hey, girls!

My name is Camy Baker, and I am what you might call an expert on popularity. Why? Because I just moved from a school where I think being popular was *the* most important thing: Beverly Hills Elementary.

Have you ever seen the movie *Clueless*? Or have you ever watched the show *Beverly Hills 90210*? Of course you have! I've seen *Clueless* ten or more times, and I have a big poster of Alicia Silverstone hanging in my closet. I'm pretty sick of *90210*, but I saved my autographed pictures of Ian Ziering and Luke Perry.

I traded my picture of Jason Priestley for a

really cool beach towel that my dog tore up, but that's okay, I don't live by the beach anymore.

If you've seen *Clueless* or watched *90210*, you've seen how my school was. We were younger, of course, and not even in middle school, but being popular was very, very important.

While I was at Beverly Hills Elementary, my dad worked at the electric company. We lived in a nice (but small) house on Robertson Boulevard. Other kids at my school had moms and dads who worked in the movie industry! One girl, nicknamed Kallie (her real name was very hard to pronounce), was the daughter of a prince from Saudi Arabia!

The way you dressed and how pretty you were were really important at Beverly Hills Elementary. I realized early on there was no way for me to compete with those girls.

The girls at my school had all the money in the world for clothes. A lot of them had dads who did plastic surgery. Twelve girls in the fifth grade had a nose job. At least twelve.

Do you remember that scene in the first episode of *Beverly Hills 90210*? The scene where Jennie Garth was going on and on about having a nose job over the summer? That scene inspired a lot of the other girls to have plastic surgery. Not me! There's no way I would go under a scalpel, thank you very much!

The thing that set me apart from the crowd was my personality. I like to talk, a lot. Also, I like to make people laugh. I have what my dad calls the gift of gab. My mom tries to get me to slow down because when I get on a roll I can talk your ear off!

I'm writing this book for a couple of reasons. First of all, I'm midway through my sixth-grade year at Peoria Middle School. Don't laugh, I still can't believe it myself. From Beverly Hills, California, to Peoria, Illinois? Hello!

Sometimes I think my parents are crazy, but we moved to Peoria when fifth grade ended because my dad got a better job. Things here are not as expensive as they are in Beverly Hills. We have a bigger house with a pool, though it's too cold to swim right now.

At Peoria Middle School I haven't had any problems making friends and fitting in. The reason I haven't had any trouble fitting in is because I used to go to one of the toughest schools in the country, in terms of making friends.

People in Beverly Hills are not exactly snobs, but they definitely do *not* go out of their way to be your friend. In a way you had to *make* them like you, and I was good at it.

So I said to myself: "Camy, you're an expert on popularity. Write a book to help other girls learn what you know!"

So here it is, my knowledge of How to Be Popular in the Sixth Grade.

The second reason for writing this book is more personal. I really, really miss Beverly Hills. Don't get me wrong, I'm doing well here at my new school. I was just voted the new president of the pep club! But Peoria is *not* Beverly Hills.

Writing this book helps me remember the good times I had in California. I left a lot of good friends back there. In a way, this book is for them.

I've split my book into two sections. In the first section I've come up with as many rules as I can remember learning at Beverly Hills Elementary. In some cases I used true stories, though I had to change the names of the kids so I wouldn't be sued by their rich mothers and fathers! Just kidding.

The second part of the book was inspired by

"Dear Abby." Have you ever read her in the newspaper? Sometimes I read her column and crack up! Adults can be so childish sometimes!

I remember a letter written by a woman who complained about her husband cheating on her. She asked "Dear Abby" what she should do! I just turned twelve, but, *HELLOOOOOOOO*, I know the answer to *that* one.

Inspired by "Dear Abby," I wrote letters to teachers at nearby schools and told them I was writing this book. I asked if they would have their students write down questions about the best way to make friends, or the best way to become popular.

Most of the teachers were really nice and helped me a lot. But some teachers thought it was wrong to teach kids how to be popular. I guess they just don't understand us that much, or what's important to us.

Anyway, the second part of the book contains questions asked by kids (mostly girls) that have to do with popularity. Before I answered the questions, I ran my answers past my mom and my sister, Sara (she's nineteen!), and they helped me out. Mostly I was right with my answers, though. As usual! J.k.

So girls (and boys, if you're sneaking a peek at your sister's book), here are my rules for being popular. I bet if you follow these rules your life will be noticeably better. Popularity is really easy anyway, and you probably know these rules already and don't even realize it!

At the end of the book I'm going to reveal a big secret about being popular. But DON'T READ IT RIGHT NOW! It's important to go all the way through the book first.

Okay, so on to the first rule.

part

1

one

1

forget the rules

this might seem like a weird rule to start my rules off with, but it's important. I don't want you to think you only have to take *my* advice to be popular. There are thousands of ways to become popular! But my rules are ones that I think work, and I hope you get some benefit out of them.

Think about this: If everyone did the same thing the same way, how would new things be created? What if all painters painted the same way? Or what if all writers, like me, wrote the same way?

While it's good to know the rules in life, sometimes it's just as good to break the rules if it brings you closer to being the person you really are. As long as you stay within the law, of course! J.k.

Seriously, it's really important to be your own individual self. If the rules ever take you away from being yourself, then make up your own rules. You know why? It's because of rule number two:

2
don't follow trends— set them!

When you imitate someone else, you know what you're doing? You're making them seem bigger than you. You're making yourself seem like a follower.

There was a girl, whom I will call Regan, in my second-period class. Her father was very wealthy, and she could buy anything she wanted. She would spend a whole afternoon with her best friend, Katy, at the Beverly Center, and her mom would leave her with a credit card! Can you believe it?

Okay, so this is bad enough, but it gets worse. Not only would Regan buy, let's say, a $240 jacket (usually in very strange colors),

11

but she would also come into class and brag about how much it cost. I get an allowance, but it would take me six months to save up that kind of money!

Regan would always ask me what I thought of her new clothes. I could tell she enjoyed seeing how jealous I was.

And get this. The following week, no fewer than five other girls would come to school on Monday morning wearing the EXACT SAME JACKET!!! It drove me crazy! So this went on for half a year. Then I finally wised up.

I said to myself, "Camy, there is no way you can compete with these girls. And you're driving yourself crazy with jealousy thinking about it!" So I hatched a plan that was brilliant, I must admit.

I started spending weekends at thrift stores. There are a lot of them in Los Angeles where they sell really old clothes for fairly cheap. But the best and most inexpensive thrift stores are in Long Beach (a very cute city about thirty minutes from L.A.—where the *Queen Mary* is docked!).

At the thrift stores I could spend twenty dollars and get some really interesting (maybe even a little strange) clothes. Once I got the clothes home, my mom would help me alter them.

With the shirts I might rip off the sleeves because I'm really into sleeveless shirts. If I bought a cardigan sweater, I would take off the buttons and put cooler ones on. Jeans I would either cut off into shorts or put interesting patches on.

My favorite things to buy were shoes, and it was my shoes that I bet most people in Beverly Hills would remember about me. If you asked them, "What is the most unique thing you can remember about Camy?" they would probably say, "She wore really crazy shoes!"

Anyway, after that first weekend of thrift shopping, I went to school on Monday morning and had to sit through Regan's story about what famous celebrity she saw at the Beverly Center that weekend. (I think she said it was the artist formerly known as Prince, to which I say, "Big deal.")

Of course Regan was showing off her new outfit and bragging about how much it cost. She even showed us the credit card receipts, which she signed herself and everything!

Then with a sneer Regan asked me what I'd done over the weekend. I was waiting for her to ask. I simply moved my feet out from under the desk and showed her my thrift shoes—red ruby slippers like the ones Dorothy wore in *The Wizard of Oz*.

Regan finally took the time to look at my whole outfit—I had on blue jeans with a really cool KROQ (a rock station) patch on the leg and was wearing a red angora sweater. In a word, I looked *FIERCE*! Then, to make a point, I told her all this cost $20.

Everyone else was really excited about how creative I had been. And I am not kidding, the next week *six* girls came back to class wearing all these crazy clothes they bought at thrift stores.

I, Camy Baker, started a trend! The trend, like most trends, did not last long, and all the girls went back to copying Regan. But I learned something about myself in the process.

So my point is, be creative and use some courage and buy that old ratty shirt from Goodwill. Take it home and have your mom alter it for you (or learn to sew yourself!) and add a blazer. You'll be killing two birds with one stone (not that I advocate killing of any sort!) by having a large wardrobe and setting yourself apart from the crowd.

And those who are *away* from the crowd get noticed!

Before I go on to the next rule, I'd like to stop here for a moment and say something about popularity. What is it, really? There are several types of popularity:

Maybe you're the prettiest girl in the class.

Maybe you're dating the cutest boy in the class.

Maybe you're the funniest girl in the class.

Maybe your best friend is the prettiest girl in the class.

But you know what?

What if next year you're not the prettiest girl in class?

What if next year you're not dating the cutest boy in class?

What if next year there's a girl even funnier than you in your class?

What if you're no longer friends with the prettiest girl in class?

See what I'm saying? All these types of popularity depend on something that could change.

You could go from being the most popular girl in class to being just like all the other girls.

You want to know what the best kind of popularity is? First, let me see if you can guess. Pick the statement you think is most true:

1. The best kind of popularity is when other kids admire you because you have a lot of money.

2. The best kind of popularity is when other kids like you because you dress cool.

3. The best kind of popularity is when everyone knows who you are and they like talking to you.

If you picked number 3, you're 1000% correct. You know why the best kind of popularity is when everyone knows who you are and they like talking to you? Because it means they think you're a friend. It means they think you're someone who is nice. No one but *you* can take that away from you. As long as you're nice, people will like you.

Regan has the kind of popularity that has to do with money and looks. But my sister, Sara, told me Regan was going to have a hard time in high school. In high school (especially Beverly Hills High School) the competition between the other girls is *FIERCE*! And Sara said Regan was going to have a hard time keeping her friends if she didn't watch it, because Regan was not a very nice person.

Now, maybe Regan will grow out of being self-centered, or maybe not. My vote is no. She just doesn't have *any* reason to be nice. Once she's finished with one best friend, she can move on to the next.

But for mere mortal girls like me (and probably you), the one thing we have to ingrain into our heads is the next rule:

be the nicest person
in your class

You might think this is pretty obvious, but being nice is something that's very easy to forget. It means being nice to everybody in your class regardless of who's popular and who's not.

Being nice involves a lot of things. I'll get to some of the finer points of being nice later, but the most important part of being nice is being kind.

Kindness is that thing you show to babies. It means being gentle and sweet and honest and careful. It doesn't mean being weak, and it doesn't mean being a follower.

Being nice means saying hello to everyone

18

you see in the hall, and it means helping someone with their homework if they ask for your
help. In fact, it means keeping an eye out for
anyone who might need your help.

It might even be a teacher who needs help,
but being nice doesn't stop with your classmates.

Being nice is like a muscle, really. You have
to work it out for it to get stronger, and the
more you work it out, the stronger it becomes.
Pretty soon you'll be so nice you won't even
have to think about it!

I have to admit something. In fourth grade,
there was a girl named Becky who was from
Texas, and I used to make fun of her. I used to
laugh at her accent. I also used to make fun of
the funky clothes she wore. Like Wranglers! She
didn't even own a pair of Levi's!

I even used to make fun of her name. Now
she goes by Rebecca, which is kind of sad because *now* I think Becky is a cool name. It's
kind of unique. But at the time, I used to make
fun of her. Who was *I* to laugh?

My first year at Beverly Hills Elementary,
the second grade, wasn't very easy either. My
classmates used to make fun of me because my
dad worked at the electric company. They used

to say that if you touched me you'd get electrocuted! It was very mean, so I guess that's why I picked on Becky.

Although I was mean, I grew out of it. Yet I feel guilty all the time for the way I treated Becky. You'll make it easier on yourself if you just try to be nice, period.

So learn from me, Camy Baker—being nice is easier is than being mean. There's less guilt involved. *Trust* me.

4

talk, talk, talk

Obviously this rule is very near and dear to my heart! But this rule is important because some girls like to blend in and pretend they're not there.

Sara says in high school at dances they called the shy boys and girls standing in the shadows wallflowers. Are you a wallflower? It's okay if you are. But it's also important to learn that it's okay to talk to people.

Now, I'm not saying you need to talk about nothing to just anybody! There are other rules attached to this rule (like all rules, really, if you think about it). But something to remember is that you've been provided with vocal cords and

21

all those things that make words possible. Animals don't have these things, *we* do.

It does you no good to sit in the back of the class and let everyone else do all the talking! How are you ever going to become popular? I for one have never heard of *silent* popularity.

And this talk, talk, talk rule is very important especially when you're around boys. Some boys have this problem that they think everything they say is really important, so you'd better listen.

There was a boy in my gym class named Chad, and he talked more than I talked. I know, I know, you're thinking that's not possible, but it's true. The bad thing about it was he talked, but he never listened! I learned a big lesson from him.

Chad talked so much you were pretty much forced to listen. I noticed that when he was around, he was the only one doing the talking. I used to listen to him, too, but then I realized Chad talked the most because other people *let* him!

Boys are like this—they think they're stronger than girls, so when they talk, they think we should listen. I say, *Snap!* My name is

Camy Baker, and it's my right to talk. (I talk in my sleep, that's how much I talk!) And I don't like seeing boys doing all the talking in gym. They're loud and unruly, but they have no right to make *any* of us girls be quiet.

Talk, girls, talk!

learn one new word a week

if you're going to talk, you'd better have something to say.

Let's face it. Popularity involves communication. Pretend for a moment you're Sandra Bullock. Now pretend you don't have any words to say. How are you going to give an interview? How are you going to talk to your fans?

This rule has a lot to do with *keeping* popularity, too. I can promise you that if you're popular, you talk to a lot of people throughout your day.

Let me throw some words out at you: *Sublime. Petulant. Grandiose. Reticent. Pointedly. Indignant. Acrimonious.*

Pretty impressive words, eh? Trust me, I barely know what they mean. But I know a really good way to help you learn the definitions. It's the way *I* learned and it must be working because, hey, look at me! I'm writing a book!

The first thing I do is go through the dictionary and look for words that I think are pretty, like *sublime. That* is a gorgeous word. If it were a boy, it would be . . . Brad Pitt. You get what I'm saying?

Anyway, after I make a list of words I like, I pretend I'm being asked a bunch of questions by Connie Chung, a famous television reporter. Well, first I have to pretend I'm a famous actress and there's a reason for Connie to want to talk with me. Then I pretend she's asking me a bunch of questions.

The first question goes like this: "So, Camy, describe to me in your own words what it was like to work with Claire Danes on your number one hit movie *How to Be Popular in the Sixth Grade*?"

"Oh, Connie," I gush, "it was *sublime*! Claire was just perfect in her role, don't you think? She'll win an Oscar for this role, I just know it!"

"So tell me, Camy," Connie asks, "were the reports about the two of you fighting over script differences the truth, or just rumors?"

"Connie," I say with a little displeasure in my voice, "you know I love Claire to death and I will not say anything bad because Camy Baker don't dish dirt!"

I realize I scolded her pretty harshly. "I don't mean to appear *petulant*. But Claire is like a big sister, so I'm very protective."

"I didn't mean to offend you, Camy. But considering this is only your first movie, don't you think you're being a bit . . . *grandiose*?"

The fact that she used the word before *I* could riles me. "That is *my* word for the day, Connie Chung, and I do not appreciate you using it before I have the chance to!"

She senses my irritation and breaks for a commercial.

After the commercial break, Connie does her best to butter me up with sweet talk. I can sense this, however, so I am now the *reticent* star.

"So Camy. Tell me. What were you like as a child?"

"I *am* a child," I tell Connie *pointedly*. She seems a bit flustered by this comment, so I back off. "Sorry, Connie. I'm still new at this interviewing business. Forgive me if I seem a bit *indignant*."

The interview ends. To show there are no bad feelings after such an *acrimonious* exchange, Connie takes me to lunch and then we go shopping.

See how fun that was? How could I ever have given such a unique interview without those words? Every single word, I found in the dictionary. After I found the word, I tried to put it into a sentence the best way I could. Try it, you'll love it.

But I must warn you about words. If you don't know their true meaning and you use the words around someone who does, you risk looking silly if you pronounce or use the words incorrectly. Try to know the words real well before you use them.

I have a very tragic example to share with you regarding the use of a word without knowing the meaning.

You've heard of Alanis Morrisette, right? If not, clue into the nineties, please! J.k.

Anyway, Alanis had a very popular song in 1996. The song was called "Ironic," and she got a lot of bad press because many people thought she used the word *ironic* incorrectly. I personally think Alanis came very close to using the word correctly. I admire her for trying to use the word to begin with!

Pray you're never in a situation like Alanis. She sold, like, over ten billion records, and a lot of those ten billion people made fun of her for using the word in a way they didn't think was proper.

I guess my point is—know the word, then use it. But *learn* the word. Whichever word. A new, pretty word. You'll need it for the next rule:

be charming

first, let me define *charming* for you.

According to my thesaurus, being charming is similar to being pleasing to the eye or mind, sweet, lovely, pretty, attractive, magnetic, fascinating, appealing, enchanting, engaging, captivating, fetching, winsome, alluring, bewitching, entrancing, prepossessing, winning. Whew!

You know what's funny? Usually when we think of the word *charming*, we think of *Prince* Charming. You know, the boy who is supposed to come into your life and sweep you off your feet?!

Well, if you're tired of waiting for Prince

Charming, like me, then I say become *Princess* Charming and do some sweeping yourself!

To me the most important things you need to be if you want to be charming are as follows:

1. Pleasing to the eye—goes with rule # 2. You don't have to wear a $240 jacket to be pleasing to the eye. You merely need to develop your own personal style and keep yourself well groomed. *Then* you'll be pleasing to the eye.

2. Sweet—fits with rule # 3. Remember when I said you should be the nicest person in class? Remember when I said niceness is like that thing you show babies—gentleness? Being sweet basically means being the nicest person in class and *meaning* it! Being sweet is being sincere.

3. Fascinating—You know how you can be fascinating? If you learn one new word a week and you use the word in the right way, at the right time, that makes you appear fascinating to kids who don't know the word yet.

Warning! Warning!

Never, *ever* use your words to make yourself seem smarter than everyone else. Use your words to help yourself appear fascinating and intelligent.

4. Engaging—Being engaging basically means what I told you was the most important type of popularity: When you're engaging, people like to talk to you and they think you're a friend.

Now that I've gotten a few of the rules out of the way, I'd like to take a moment and tell you who my most favorite hero is in this great big world of ours.

This girl is my hero because in a way, she is the most popular girl in our country. In my view she is the kind of girl we should all strive to become. She is smart and feisty (she has a lot of money, too, but that's just icing!), and her name is Chelsea Clinton.

Chelsea Clinton represents a kind of popularity that's very rare, but something all of us girls dream about.

The Chelsea Clinton type of popularity

31

happens when a girl from a very high-profile family (her father's the President, of course) becomes known to everybody, and actually appears *nice*!

Now, I don't know Chelsea personally. Maybe after my book tour (if it ever happens!) I'll get a chance to meet her. But from what I've seen so far, she is sweet and charming and smart!

The most important thing that Chelsea teaches girls like us is that it doesn't matter *who* your father is—you still have to be a good person. Chelsea is kind of like my friend Brooke in Beverly Hills.

Brooke's father owns a bank, that's how rich they are. You'd think Brooke would be the most selfish, stuck-up person you'd ever met. But Brooke was actually the one who inspired a lot of these rules.

Ever since second grade, Brooke and I lived close to each other—her home was a mansion, mine just a split-level ranch. Through some strange coincidence, our homes were in the same neighborhood.

Brooke would walk me home, and she liked coming inside because my mom was always cooking something or other. Brooke liked the smell of fresh-baked cookies. I guess her live-in nanny cooked a lot, but Brooke liked seeing my mom in the kitchen for some reason.

While Brooke and I were never "best friends," Brooke always took the time to help me fit in at Beverly Hills Elementary, ever since the second grade. She always gave me good advice.

Once, when a big school dance was coming up and my mom wouldn't buy me the outfit I wanted, Brooke loaned me the money to buy it. I paid her back. With a dollar interest!

Brooke was my buddy. In a way she was like a sister. I respected and admired her because she was so down-to-earth.

Chelsea reminds me of Brooke. While Chelsea and I probably would never be best friends (she is a lot older, after all!), I could see myself hanging out with her, or going through her closet.

Chelsea Clinton is what all of us new nineties girls should shoot for. We should be nice and humble, and most importantly, we should make our mothers stress out about which college we want to go to! J.k.

Okay, now it's time for me to get a little serious here. On to the next very important rule:

seek advice

i have to admit my mom encouraged me to write this one, and when she explained it better to me I agreed with her 1000%.

See, some of you out there reading this book right now might be in a situation that's very hard. It could be that your parents are splitting up. Or maybe you're having a hard time in school. Maybe the problem is much worse. Maybe you feel like you're the only person in the world going through a certain problem.

The first thing I want to say is that whatever problem you're facing, it is *not* your fault. Whatever it is, it doesn't have anything to do with you.

Some kids *seem* to have everything, with no problems or anything. But that's just not the case. We all have one problem or another, and some problems are bigger than others, but the only way for us to be able to get a grip on our problems is to talk about them.

It's great if you have a best friend you feel comfortable talking about your problems with. But for the very big problems, when you need very good advice, I suggest you talk to your school counselor.

The school counselors are men and women who are paid to listen to kids like you and me and guide us through the difficult moments.

It's your right to speak with the counselors, and they should always make the time to chat with you. This means using the fourth rule, though. You have to talk and tell them what the problem is for them to help you.

If you have a problem and don't talk about it, that might lead to another problem, which brings me to the next rule:

don't bottle it up

regina was in my gym class. She always looked so sad, sometimes I just wanted to run up to her and give her a hug. Though I got the feeling she wouldn't have liked it.

I found out only later that Regina's mother was sick through our whole fifth-grade year and passed away before the summer. Regina never said anything! I knew in my heart, though, something was wrong.

In gym Regina would snap at the teacher for no reason at all, and she would be sent to detention after school, making things worse.

See, if Regina had just told someone what she was going through, maybe the gym teacher,

36

Mrs. Parker, would have better understood how to handle the situation.

Instead, Regina bottled up everything she was feeling. That bottle could only hold so much before it *burst*. That's why we call them *outbursts*! They seem to come out of the blue, but really it's just too much for one bottle to hold.

The bottle can hold just about anything, too. There are lots of problems out there, and if you're going through one, don't hold it in.

choose your mirrors carefully

You've been to a carnival, right? Remember the fun house, with all the wacky mirrors? There was one mirror that made you look short and chubby. The other mirror made you look thin and tall. Other mirrors made you look like an alien!

Remember this: People are like mirrors.

Some people make you feel very good about yourself. Usually these people accept you for who you are. You don't feel the need to compete with them, and they *never* put you down.

Other people make you feel bad about yourself. Usually these people are very critical of your appearance, or they make fun of you. After they say something mean, they'll usually say "Just kidding" so you don't get mad.

But if someone you trust says something that's not nice about or to you, you tend to believe them. They are your mirror, and you trust them.

You know what? You can't trust mirrors! You know why? Mirrors don't reflect things accurately! What's worse, you can't even trust the mirror in the bathroom!

Let me explain something here: One day you can go into the bathroom and look at yourself in the mirror. Maybe it's gloomy outside and no light is coming into the bathroom. You look at yourself in the mirror and you feel like you don't look so good. You know why? There's not enough light! We all look better in light!

Or maybe after a big Thanksgiving dinner you go into the bathroom and look at your stomach and say to yourself, "Oh my God, I am so fat!" You know what? You only look fat because you *feel* fat. You did not get fat in the twenty minutes it took you to eat that turkey, stuffing, rolls and, if they're your things, yams and cranberry sauce.

The only true mirror you will ever have is the one *within* you.

There is a mirror in our heads, and Sara told me what to call it: self-perception. You might think you don't look into that mirror, but everyone does.

If your self-perception is bad, you say or believe things like "I'm fat," "I'm ugly," "My nose is too big." Either someone planted those thoughts in your head or you created them yourself, but either way you should not believe those things.

If your self-perception is good, you say things like "I am pretty," "I like my body," "I am smart," "I am a great person."

You need the *good* thoughts. You need the good self-perception. You need people around you who support the good thoughts.

Camellia and I were best friends the beginning of my fifth-grade year. Camellia is a very pretty girl and she's very smart, though we grew apart later in the year because, to tell you the truth, she started depressing me.

Camellia was not fat, but she thought she was, and she thought everyone else thought she was fat.

One day I asked, "Camellia, just *who* told you that you're fat?" Camellia said it was her brother. I about choked on my yogurt. "Your brother? The boy who scarfs down your hamburger and mine whenever we go to Jack in the Box? *That* brother?" I asked.

"Yeah," she said weakly.

It made me so mad, I couldn't believe it! Camellia's brother Freddie called *her* fat!

And what was worse was that Freddie made Camellia believe she was fat. Camellia only wore baggy clothes (a year before they were in style!), and she never went to the public pool.

Camellia never went to the beach unless she wore shorts and a long T-shirt. She wasn't fat at all, but Freddie convinced her she was!

You can't believe *anything* bad that someone says about you. No one has the right to pick on you. No one has the right to make you feel bad about yourself. What *we* believe about ourselves is *the* most important thing.

Even if we don't think we're thin, pretty, or smart, we just have to believe we *are* those things. Maybe we *will* become them if we're not already there. Do you see what I'm saying? Imagine the qualities you want and they'll find you—as long as you look into that good mirror in *yourself*.

10

be independent

One day in fifth grade a group of my best friends and I were standing around our lockers. It was the day before pep squad try-outs. My friend Kim saw Ericka and said, "Ericka, you should try out with us!" And Ericka said, "No, no, I need more time to study." After Ericka walked away, Kim said, "Or you mean Dirk won't let you." Dirk was Ericka's boyfriend.

Another time my friend Kallie and I were to go shopping at the Beverly Center over the weekend, and we invited Michelle to come along with us. Michelle was still pretty new to the school, and we hadn't had a chance to bond with her. Well, Michelle turned us down. She said she was busy.

Later Kallie and I learned that Michelle's friend Stephanie had told her not to go. The reason? Stephanie doesn't like Kallie. She thinks Kallie is stuck-up. Kallie is the furthest thing from stuck-up—Stephanie is just jealous. Michelle didn't want to risk making Stephanie mad, so she didn't go with us.

Have you ever heard this phrase from your boyfriend?: "No one will ever like you as much as me." Barf! Or maybe you've heard this from your "best" friend: "You'll never find a better friend than me." Gag.

Get clues, everyone, okay? While we're still kids, we're about to become teenagers, and we don't need to play these little games.

We're all strong enough and capable enough and mature enough to be self-sufficient. Part of being self-sufficient is being independent enough to make our own choices and take responsibility for our actions.

You don't need a boy to make you feel special or pretty. Remember my rule about the mirrors? If you follow that rule, the only person you'll need to feel pretty is yourself.

You don't need a "friend" to tell you which girls you can hang around with. Maybe your parents can, if you tend to hang around with people who aren't good for you, but no one else can tell you what to do.

Girls, it's time for us to wake up and smell the CK One!

I'm not saying break up with your boyfriend if you suspect he fits the above description. And I'm not saying you should stop being friends with a girl who tries to run your life.

What I'm saying is that *you* are responsible for *you*. No boy or girl should be depended on to make you feel secure. No one owes you anything, and no one can give you anything. If you depend on other people to make you happy, then you're dependent upon them.

"Be independent" is an important rule to start using now, before you grow older and it gets harder and harder to do. We all have the ability to make our *own* selves happy. That means being nice, of course, and doing all the other things I've mentioned. But it also means learning to do things for yourself. Okay? Okay. On we go.

11

ask questions

this is kind of like the talk, talk, talk rule, but not really. When you talk, you don't necessarily have to have a purpose in mind. You can talk about clothes or boys or music or movies or anything.

But a question has a purpose: You need to know something.

Questions are sometimes frightening to ask because you might think you're not smart if you ask them. I'm here to tell you that the only way you're going to learn anything is if you ask questions.

I always ask questions, and I always have. My dad says "But why?" are the first words that came out of my mouth. My dad suggested that I include this rule because he said it's a great habit to have and it will help me get smarter and smarter.

If you ever come across something that you don't understand, ask a question. Ask your parents, ask a teacher, ask a counselor, ask a friend. If they don't know the answer and can't find it for you, look it up in an encyclopedia at school, or in the dictionary if it's a word you don't understand. (This could be one of the words you learn in a week!)

Never take "Because I said so" as an answer for anything. If you ever hear "Because I said so" from anyone, ask someone else the question.

Trust me, I had a *lot* of questions when my parents said we were moving to Peoria. I didn't know why I had to leave my friends, so I asked my mom why we couldn't just stay in Beverly Hills.

"Camy," she said, "when your father gets a new opportunity, *you* get an opportunity as well. He wants more than anything to send you to college, and this move will help him further along that goal."

"How?" I asked angrily. College was, like, a

decade away or something, and all I knew was that I was going to miss all my friends more than I cared about college.

"But college is very expensive. He's working toward a goal in his career with the hope that we can give you the best education, like the one we're giving Sara."

It took me a while, and a few hundred more questions, to finally come to terms with the move. In a way, the move was good. (It actually gave birth to another rule you'll read later!) Anyway, I could have easily just accepted my fate without asking any questions, and I might have resented my parents for the move. But now I accept it. They helped me understand.

Questions help you discover new things. Asking a question is like moving to a new city—you get to see a different part of the world.

A lot of kids, and I *know* a lot of them, don't even bother to ask questions about the things they are unclear about. They just assume they know the answer to everything. Boy, do I know from experience how wrong they are, which leads me to the next rule:

12

you don't know it all,
so don't pretend to

you've heard the phrase (and hopefully it was not directed at you) "Little Ms. Know-It-All."

There was this girl in my school . . . Okay, actually this girl was me. Yes, I, Camy Baker, was once crowned by kids in my class Little Ms. Know-It-All.

It was second grade, and I was still trying to fit in. I've already told you how tough it was to fit in at Beverly Hills Elementary, plus I've told you my parents were not rich. Nothing was distinguishing me from the rest of the girls. I was lost in the crowd.

So I became the best student in my class. Now, that would have been great, if I had just

48

excelled at my studies. Uh-uh, not enough for greedy old me! I had to act like I knew *everything*.

At recess I took it upon myself to show the other girls how to jump rope. I learned how to jump rope when we lived in Philadelphia, the place we lived before moving to Beverly Hills. All the girls at recess were impressed that I knew how to jump so well, and I guess I was a little too proud of my ability and became a show-off.

No one dared argue about jump rope with Camy Baker, because *snap*, I knew it all. Well, it was true, no one argued with me. But, sadly, soon no one talked to me.

Then I started to hear the rumors: "There goes Little Ms. Know-It-All."

I must admit, at first I thought they were complimenting me. That's how superior I felt.

Here's a good test of whether you are a Little Ms. Know-It-All. Answer the following questions with a yes or no:

1. When someone tells a funny story, do you like to tell an even *better* one after they're done?

2. Have you found that your classmates have stopped asking for your opinion about things?

3. If you're asked a question but don't know the answer, do you answer it anyway?

If you answered yes to all three of the above questions, I'm afraid to say you're a Little Ms. Know-It-All. But don't despair, the way out of this predicament is easy, and the reason you got to this point is not your fault.

The reason I was a Little Ms. Know-It-All was because I was insecure. Maybe your reason is because you really do know a lot and like to show off. Or maybe you always want to be the center of attention.

As I've learned, you don't always have to be the center of attention.

In the fourth grade there was a girl named Tif who was very hungry for the limelight, if you know what I mean. She thought she knew everything, plus she had a story for every occasion. When Tif was around, we could never say anything because she always thought she had a better story. We all called her Attention Tif.

Fighting to be the center of attention is not a good way to become popular. It's really just begging. It annoys you when your dog begs for food, right? Well, you're just as annoying if you beg for attention.

Now, I don't want any of you to read this rule and start scouting around like a nosy neighbor: Is she a know-it-all, is she? The point to this rule is to help a girl who always has to be the center of attention find a way out of her predicament. And the best way to get away from being a know-it-all or attention-grabber is to follow the next rule:

13

be humble

this rule might be the most important in terms of *staying* popular. And if you're a Little Ms. Know-It-All or have made people mad because you always have to be the center of attention, it might be the rule you most need to learn in order to feel better about yourself. And what have I already said? The most important thing is that you feel good about yourself.

Let me talk from experience. One day in second grade I heard a group of girls say, "There goes Little Ms. Know-It-All." Remember I said I thought they were complimenting me?

I went home and told my mom that all the

girls at school liked me because I knew every-thing. I told my mom what they called me.

I can still remember the look on my mom's face. I saw it clearly the day she thought she lost me at the Beverly Center when I went off to look at some patent leather shoes. It was the same look. I knew it wasn't good. But she didn't say anything right away.

That night my mom and dad talked—I could hear their voices, but despite the glass cup to the wall I couldn't make out what they were saying.

Later my mom came into my room and sug-gested I have a party for my birthday. She said we would make special invitations and invite all the girls in my class! And we would have cake and ice cream. I thought I was in heaven. (Remember—I was only in second grade!)

The girls came to my party, but they basi-cally ate my cake and ice cream and then left. They brought presents, of course (this was Beverly Hills, after all!), but they only stayed an hour at the most. No one invited me to the pool party I overheard was happening later in the day. I was crushed.

My mom later told me she'd suggested the party for a reason—she wanted to see how I acted around the other girls. I guess what she saw clued her in to what the other girls thought of me.

That night my mom and I had a long talk. She explained to me why people were treating me as if they didn't like me. She said I needed to learn an important lesson in my life. That lesson's name is the rule above: "Be humble."

Humble rhymes with *bumble,* so if you ever forget the word, think of a bumblebee. Being humble means being like a bumblebee! J.k.

Being humble is being gracious. Being gracious means being kind and courteous. It means you appreciate things and are thankful for them. It means accepting your unique gifts without bragging about them. Being humble basically means you realize you're no better or worse than anyone else.

We're all human beings. We all eat, breathe, and sleep. While we're different in a lot of ways, ultimately we are all equal.

Now, if I can learn this in Beverly Hills, where there aren't many girls from middle-class families like me, then *you* can learn this.

It doesn't matter what you wear, what you know, whom you know, or where you live. No one is any better or worse than you.

Basically, if you treat other people with kindness and respect and don't think you're better or worse than anybody, then you'll be humble.

14

be the smartest
person in your class

now that I've explained about the Little Ms. Know-It-All syndrome, I think it's safe to put this rule out there without anyone getting carried away! Because part of being smart is knowing when to show your intelligence and when to be humble about it.

You know who Cindy Crawford is, right? She is, like, the most beautiful woman in the whole world. But you want to know something interesting about Cindy Crawford? She was once a valedictorian, and she was going to study chemistry in college before she went on to become a supermodel.

Being smart basically means applying yourself to your studies. It doesn't mean you have to get an A on every test. It just means you have to try your hardest.

Sara tells me that popularity comes in waves. One year a girl is extremely popular. The next year she isn't. Or the most popular crowd in elementary school doesn't even register on the popularity Richter scale in middle school.

Often, Sara says, a new boy or girl will come into school and knock whoever is the most popular off their pedestal. With popularity, you just never know.

So my point in this rule is that you need to have your smarts to fall back on. Cindy Crawford didn't know for sure she was going to be a supermodel. You don't know for sure you're going to be really popular. And even if you are, you still need to be smart to get into college.

Even if we don't fully believe it now, there's more to life than being popular.

I personally like being popular. But I agree that there's got to be more to a girl than just a friendly face and a few kind words.

So being the smartest person in the class basically boils down to trying your hardest. If you try your hardest, you're being smart—because your effort is going to pay off with all the great things you know.

15

stand tall

Your mom probably tells you all the time, just like my mom, "Sit up straight!" Well, pretend I'm your mom for a sec: "Stand up straight!" You know why? The higher you stand, the more people look up to you.

There was this girl in my third-period class, Kimberly, who slouched wherever she walked. She looked like she wanted to crawl into herself, she was so shy and frightened. I'll bet you anything that unless she reads this book and sees herself in what I'm describing, she's going to go through her school years like a broken flower or something.

Standing straight and sitting straight are not

only good for your back. Really, I'm giving you this advice because your body gives off many clues about your personality. If you think I'm kidding, notice what your body is saying next time you sit next to a person you don't like.

Pretend you're in the school auditorium. And pretend your teacher makes you sit next to a really gross boy who insists on putting very nasty things from his nose under the seat in front of him.

Of *course* you want to get as far away from him as possible! But since you can't roam around during the speech or play or whatever it is, you have to sit there.

I can guarantee you'll be sitting with your legs shifted as far away from this gross kid as possible. Your shoulders and head and everything else will be nearly touching the person in the seat next to you. (Pray it's not another gross kid!)

My point is, your body language will say at that moment what you feel about the gross kid next to you. In the same way, how you hold yourself tells people whether you're confident, shy, awkward, or clumsy.

To put out the right body language, all you

have to do is feel confident. The easiest way to do that is to think and stand tall. And, girls, we might feel just as tall as boys now, but in the next few years they're going to grow a *lot* taller than we will grow.

We need to start feeling tall now before we have one of those boys standing over us, waving nasty fingers in our faces! *Gross!*

be yourself

the only thing you own is yourself. That's it. You're born into this world with yourself, and when you leave this world, you leave yourself behind.

Isn't that weird to think about? The only thing you will ever really have is you. You, you, you!

You know what? There's not another person in this world exactly like you. Nowhere, nohow, no way. You are individual, special, and unique.

That's scary, isn't it? We all feel different at one time or another, don't we? Usually we think it's a bad thing to be different, but really our differences are what make us individual, special, and unique.

Being yourself requires nothing but courage. Being yourself means not doing what your friends are doing if it doesn't feel right.

If you can see shades of other rules in this rule, then you see correctly. Being yourself is most similar to "don't follow trends—set them." But "yourself" is not a trend. "Yourself" is yours to keep. And despite what you might think, being yourself has a lot to do with popularity.

When you follow this rule, if you can be yourself, then you'll feel better about yourself. And what is it that I keep saying? If you feel good about yourself, others will feel good about *you*. This concept is the basis of popularity. You feel good, others feel good, you all feel happy.

Let me give you a few examples of when you're not being yourself.

Not being yourself is when you kiss your boyfriend if you don't want to.

Not being yourself is when you shoplift because a friend wants you to do it. (Trust me, I have seen this shoplifting thing enough to take it seriously. Girls do it all the time, and most regret it. But they almost always say, "Well, So-and-so was doing it.")

Not being yourself is taking a drink of your parents' beer when your older sister's friends are doing it. (Sara doesn't drink, but I was imagining a scenario if she did!)

You know why it's important to be "you" now? If you're not yourself now, if you follow other people or fail to stand by what you know is true, you might lose that special something that makes you you. And "you" is harder to find the more you pretend to be something you're not, or do something you don't want to do.

Do you want to know how you'll know when you're ready to do something? It will *feel* right. You won't have to say things like "What if we get caught?" Or "What if we get caught?" Or "What if we get caught?" You get my point?

There are so many creative ways to be yourself, and the best of them don't give you that sinking, scared feeling in your stomach.

Do you want to know the best way to be yourself? I hope so, 'cause it's the next rule!

17

develop a talent

my sister, Sara, is in her first year of college. She's having a hard time in her French class. A lot of the students are having a difficult time with French.

The French professor told Sara and her classmates to go home and pound this thought into their younger brothers' and sisters' heads: Develop or learn a talent *now* because things are easier to learn when you're young.

Have you ever wondered why gymnasts, tennis players, and singers are so much better when they start young? Sara says it's because when we're young, we're not afraid of trying something new.

Isn't that funny? But it's true. How many adults do you know who practice gymnastics? Not many. Partly it's because their bones aren't as supple as ours, but it's also because as you get older, the thought of doing a back flip is terrifying. But to us it's not a huge deal.

Sara says it gets harder to learn new things as you get older, because you become afraid of failing.

So, if you like to paint, start painting. If you like to sing, start singing. If you like to play the piano, start playing.

Sara wants to go to Paris for a summer, and she guarantees that I'll want to go there when I get older too.

I don't know if I can juggle writing and studying French, but I'm going to give it my best effort. I'd like to try gymnastics as well, but I'm afraid that with school, writing, pep club, and everything else, I won't have time.

I have to tell you something. Developing a talent is not easy. Sometimes it's downright frustrating because it takes you away from other activities. But trust me, girls. The mall is not going anywhere. There will be other parties.

Sometimes you might feel that developing a talent takes up too much of your time. This leads me to the next rule. But, before we go there, I want to take a detour for just a bit.

"tour de force"
a short story

"tour de Force" is a fantasy about a girl named Camy Baker who lives in an alternative universe. She's only twelve, but she drives a red BMW with a sunroof. (No convertibles, please—it takes a long time to curl my hair!)

The new No Doubt tape is playing full blast in the CD player—ha, ha, just trying to see if you're still awake. The new No Doubt CD is playing full blast in the CD player.

Camy drives down Sunset Boulevard in the red BMW, wearing a great big silk scarf to protect the curls. The scarf flows out the sunroof, whipping in the wind. In a word, Camy looks *FIERCE*!

It's a gorgeous day. The sun blazes over the City of Angels, and Camy knows that everyone, everywhere, looks good.

This is sort of a homecoming for Camy, a chance to celebrate her tour de force. She has spent a whole year away from the school in Beverly Hills she attended for four years. She's eager to see her old friends.

Normally, Camy can't drive because she's only twelve, but her parents rented her this incredibly sassy car for this special occasion (this is a fantasy, don't forget!).

Camy pulls up to a Beverly Hills mansion, and none other than Keanu Reeves is there to park her car!

Camy tosses Keanu the keys with a slight smile, and she thinks she hears him whistle, but it could just be the Santa Ana winds rustling through the stiff and creaky palm trees.

Camy walks into the mansion, and Brad Pitt is there to take her scarf! It's amazing to Camy that such a big star is doing the hat-check thing, so she says something. "Brad, what are you doing here?"

Brad smiles like he knows all the world's

secrets. "It's your fantasy, Camy," he purrs like a cat. Then he winks.

Camy gets all tingly as Brad takes her scarf and hangs it on the coatrack, then waits for the next partygoer to arrive. Camy walks farther into the mansion.

Arnold Schwarzenegger is in the living room, and he points Camy toward the pool, but she gets the shivers because Arnold is, like, a dinosaur.

So Camy closes her eyes and imagines someone else. And there, before her, is Tom Cruise, his lopsided grin angling toward the back of the house. "The party is out by the pool, Camy, have fun."

Camy tries to say "Thank you," but she can't—she's too excited. Instead she calms the butterflies in her stomach. Then she walks outside. The pool teems with the bodies of her friends. There's Rachel . . . and Kimberly . . . and Kallie! *Everyone* is there! Even Chad, who is talking Keisha's ear off!

Camy stands there watching her friends, and an incredible sadness comes over her. She hadn't realized how much she missed these people—her friends, the inspiration for her highly successful and megaselling book, *How to Be Popular in the Sixth Grade*.

No one sees Camy yet, and that's good. If she wore makeup, Camy would have to rush to the bathroom, because she's crying and mascara would be running down her face!

But Camy simply wipes the tears away and prepares to meet her dear old friends.

Out of the corner of her eye, Camy notices a woman sitting on a lawn chair, reading a copy of *Vanity Fair*.

The woman looks up, her eyes hidden under sunglasses. The woman lowers the glasses, and Camy realizes with an electric shock—it's Alicia Silverstone!

"They're waiting for ya, Camy. They're all *real* proud," Alicia says with a smile.

Camy loses it! "Alicia, Alicia, I loved you in *Clueless*! Can I have your autograph? Oh my gosh, the kids back in Peoria are going to flip!!!!"

THE END

The ending of "Tour de Force" was originally going to be different, but I guess I ended my detour with a detour.

Originally I planned for "Camy" to walk down to her friends, and for them to be in awe of her for being such a famous author and everything.

"Camy" was going to soak up the attention like a sponge and spend the rest of the afternoon telling her friends about the incredible things she had done since leaving Beverly Hills.

But if you're a writer, the one thing you learn is that stories change if you're open to inspiration. I figured I would take a more humble route and end the story with "Camy's" joy at meeting one of her heroes.

I wrote this story for a couple of reasons. First, I wanted to illustrate the above rule about discovering a talent. If you think this story was fun to *read,* girls, let me tell you how fun it was to *write*!

I never would have known how fun writing was if I'd never started. But what's more, writing makes me appear fascinating to people. Kids really like the stories I write.

So, in a way, writing helps me to be popular. Not only that, but it makes me feel good about myself. It's this whole fun circle, really.

The second reason I wrote the story was to set up the next rule. As I mentioned before, developing a talent takes time away from other activities. I mean, when I write, I sit alone in my room with the door closed, working on my computer. There's no other way but to be alone. So the next rule is:

18

be by yourself—it's okay

it's Friday night. You know that out there, in the world, someone is having fun. In fact, you say to yourself: "Everyone, *everywhere* is out there having fun. Everyone but *me*, that is." Or maybe it's Saturday night and you say to yourself . . . you get my point? You feel lonely.

I can tell you from experience that the life of popularity is not as glamorous as it might seem. There are many weekends when the invitations are nonexistent.

This rule is important to know when you think about popularity, because when we kids are bored, we tend to get into trouble. Let's face it, we do. We are, as my mom says, "up to

74

no good." It's hard to be popular—which ultimately involves going to parties—if you're grounded.

Sara told me about this time just after we'd moved to Beverly Hills. She wasn't invited to a party that she really wanted to go to. So what did Sara do? She smoked a cigarette.

It sure shocked me! Sara is an advocate of vegetarianism and all other kinds of clean living. So I was very surprised to learn that because her feelings were hurt, she smoked a cigarette. Where she got it, I don't even want to know. I can just imagine her finding it on the street or something . . . *sick!*

Anyway, Sara is over that stage. Now when she's bored, she reads a book. When I'm bored, I write. I guess my point about this rule, and why it relates to popularity, is that you don't have to feel bad if you suddenly find yourself at home without anything to do. It happens to all of us.

Wait, I have a suggestion. Read a book, any book, *my* book! J.k.

19

find a friend

there's a friend for everybody out there, you know that? Even if you're shy; even if you're new to the school; even if you feel nobody in this world likes you . . . you have a friend.

Maybe you haven't yet found that friend, but he or she is waiting for you. And while you're waiting for that friend, you know what you should do? Practice these rules. Every single one of them. Be nice, talk, stand tall, blah, blah, blah.

You get my point? Maybe if you do all these things, you'll open yourself up to that friend who's waiting for you just as much as you're waiting for him or her.

Dear *Camy Baker* Reader,

We want to know what you think! Please take the time to answer the following questions *after* you have read the book. Be completely honest—there are no right or wrong answers. You don't even need a stamp; just fill out the card and drop it in the mailbox. Thanks!

1. Did you like this book? (Check one) ☐ I loved it ☐ I liked it ☐ It was OK ☐ I didn't like it ☐ I hated it

2. How did you find out about this book? (Check one) ☐ Ad in *Girls' Life* magazine ☐ Sneak preview sampler in *Girls' Life* magazine ☐ In-store display ☐ Friend ☐ Other (Please specify) _____

3. Would you read another *Camy Baker* book? (Check one) ☐ Definitely Yes ☐ Probably Yes ☐ Maybe ☐ Probably Not ☐ Definitely Not

4. Please check which of the following choices was most important to you in deciding to buy this book. (Check one) ☐ Subject/Content ☐ Cover ☐ Friend recommended ☐ Back-of-book copy ☐ Read preview sampler ☐ Advertisement

5. Would you recommend *Camy Baker* books to a friend? (Check one) ☐ Definitely Yes ☐ Probably Yes ☐ Maybe ☐ Probably Not ☐ Definitely Not

6. Where did you get this book? ☐ Waldenbooks ☐ Borders ☐ Barnes & Noble ☐ Other bookstore (Please specify) _____ ☐ Discount store (like K-Mart) ☐ Grocery store ☐ Received as a gift ☐ Other (Please specify) _____

7. Who picked out this book? (Check one) ☐ I did ☐ Friend ☐ Parent/Grandparent ☐ Other (Please specify) _____

8. On a scale of 1-10 (1 is worst, 10 is best) how does *How to Be Popular in the Sixth Grade* rank as a book? _____

9. Which, if any, of these magazines do you read regularly? (Check all that apply) ☐ *Girls' Life* ☐ *Disney Adventures* ☐ *All About You!* ☐ *American Girl* ☐ *Nickelodeon* ☐ Other(s) _____

10. Have you been to *Camy Baker's* official Web site (www.camybaker.com)? ☐ Yes ☐ Not yet ☐ No

11. If you answered Yes to question 10, on a scale of 1-10 (1 is worst, 10 is best) how would you rate *Camy Baker's* official Web site? _____

12. What sorts of features would you like to see on the *Camy Baker* Web site? (Please specify) _____

Reader's Name _____ Date of Birth ___/___/___

Address _____ City _____ State _____ Zip _____

CB1

BUSINESS REPLY MAIL

FIRST-CLASS MAIL   PERMIT NO. 01239   NEW YORK, NY

POSTAGE WILL BE PAID BY ADDRESSEE

BANTAM DOUBLEDAY DELL
BOOKS FOR YOUNG READERS
MARKETING DEPT.
1540 Broadway
New York NY 10109-1225

NO POSTAGE
NECESSARY
IF MAILED
IN THE
UNITED STATES

20

don't cling to friends, boyfriends, or popularity

One thing I've learned is that things change. Girls, I'm talking from experience here.

A year ago, if you had told me I was leaving Southern California for Illinois, I would have taken you by the hand and personally delivered you to the school nurse to have your head examined.

But here I am, in Illinois. My mom tells me this is my first big change of *many* that are sure to come.

I write to my friends in Beverly Hills, but I've made plenty of new ones here. Jackie's my best friend in Peoria. Better than *any* friend I've had *anytime* in my life, so the change was good.

Jackie's boyfriend doesn't like me, though.

He calls me a Beverly Hills snob! Can you believe it?! Me, a snob? Hardly! Oh well, boyfriends come and go (he's going, girls, *trust* me), but best friends last forever!

I haven't had a *real* boyfriend yet—I'm waiting, girls, I'm waiting—but when I do, I'm sure we're not going to date all the way through college, after which we will get married! Things change.

Okay, I admit it—I *am* one of the most popular girls in Peoria Middle School. But anything can happen in high school. Things change.

You ought to look at pictures of Sara! She was, well, a little homely in middle school. But in high school, look out! She blossomed into one of the prettiest girls I've ever seen!

What if I go in the opposite direction? I hope not!

It probably will *not* happen, but what's important is that I feel good about myself. Things, people, and situations change. But as long as I feel good about myself, the changes won't cause me any grief!

So, don't cling to anything, because when it goes away, you don't want to be sad. You want to be happy! ☺

don't be jealous of anybody!

you know why you shouldn't be jealous of anybody? There are two things you should know.

The first and most important reason you should not be jealous of a person is that it means you're not happy for them. If you aren't happy for them, then you're *unhappy* for them—☹—you get my point?

The second reason you should not be jealous of anybody is because you don't even know for sure if what they have is a *good* thing!

Wendy was jealous of Rachel because Rachel's mother was a movie star. There was nothing Wendy could do about it—she couldn't turn *her* mother into a movie star. So it was a pointless jealousy.

And if Wendy had not spent so much time *competing* with Rachel, she could have been friends with Rachel.

Rachel is really nice, but she knew that a lot of the girls were jealous of her.

I was Rachel's friend, and I personally found it fascinating that Rachel's mother was a movie star. (I'd love to tell you who her mother is, but I can't. Rachel is still a good friend, and she would never forgive me if I divulged that secret!)

Since I was a friend to Rachel, I learned something that Wendy will never know. I learned that it was very hard to be the daughter of a celebrity. Not only did weirdos try to break into their house once, but they always had people following them.

And Rachel did not see her mother very often, because she was always off at some exotic movie location.

Rachel once told me, "Wendy is so jealous of me, but I would trade for her parents in a minute!" Not that she wanted to leave her mother or anything, but Rachel didn't like the problems that went along with being the daughter of a celebrity. (And her mother is a *huge* star!)

Wendy basically wasted much of her time envying Rachel for something that isn't even that great to begin with.

Another kind of jealousy comes when someone gets something you want.

For instance, Pamela used to always get A pluses on all her tests. Every single one. No one studied as hard as Pamela, but everyone used to gripe whenever the papers were passed back and word got around that Pamela *again* had beaten everyone on the test.

Pamela handled the jealousy well, though, and no one *really* disliked her for always getting the best grades. You know why? She had quite a way with the next rule:

laugh and smile as much as humanly possible

Pamela had a thousand-watt smile. That's what my dad called it because he's in the electric business.

In Hollywood they call them million-dollar smiles. Tom Cruise and Julia Roberts have million-dollar smiles. When they smile, people go to their movies.

If you think I'm kidding about the importance of a smile, look at Julia Roberts's movie career.

When Julia Roberts smiles a lot in her movies, like she did in *Pretty Woman* and *My Best Friend's Wedding*, people go to see her movies. When Julia doesn't smile, like in that horrible *Mary Reilly*, people stay away.

Audiences don't want to see a woman with the most beautiful smile in the world looking all grim and gross. Smile, Julia, smile!

Pamela knew this secret. No one could ever be mad at Pamela. She just had that killer smile.

My mom always says, "Laugh and the world laughs with you." I used to think that if I laughed, people would laugh *at* me. Now I know what she means: Laugh and people laugh *along* with you.

Laughing is contagious. If you don't believe me, try this experiment: Rent the latest Jim Carrey movie and watch it all by yourself. Of course some parts will be funny, but generally the movie will be very bad and you'll be embarrassed for Jim, his costars, and anyone else associated with the movie.

After Part I of the experiment, wait a week, then rent the movie again. Only this time, invite a couple of friends over to watch the movie with you. Before you start the movie, do your usual girl *thang*. Talk about boys, fashion, music, etc. Then start the movie.

You saw the movie, right? You thought it was pretty lame and can't understand why everyone is talking about it.

Well, watching it with your friends, something miraculous happens. Since you're all in a good mood, you and your friends are laughing and laughing and laughing. Everything is funny. Anything Jim Carrey does is outrageous and hilarious. You can't stop laughing. Am I right?

See, what's happened is this: You and your friends are making each other laugh because you hear each other laugh and see each other laugh. You're having fun. And the movie, which you previously thought was dreadful, is the funniest movie you've ever seen because you're in a good mood and you *want* to laugh and you're letting the movie work its magic on you.

Try it if you don't believe me that laughing is contagious.

Smiling is contagious too. When you smile at someone, their first instinct, unless they're having a *really* bad day, is to smile back at you.

If they don't smile back, you know what? They're not having a good day, and there's nothing you can do but keep smiling and hope that whatever makes them sad, angry, or bitter will soon leave them.

☺ or ☹. Which do you like better?

Also, you feel different when you laugh and

when you smile. You *look* different when you laugh and smile. You look happy, and mostly, that makes people think you're someone they might like to know.

 If you ever encounter a person who says, "What's *she* so happy about?" in a negative way, that's a person to avoid. Nothing needs to be funny or exciting to make you laugh or smile. Try it, you'll like it!

23

don't do drugs

this is your brain. Thikhadfkkds is youo-jerjrkejr braidflaldldn on druglsls;g;s/ Any questions?

Seriously, being from Los Angeles, I think I was exposed to a more realistic view of drugs than most kids, except for the kids in inner cities, I guess.

My friend Rachel (remember, her mother is a movie star) told me that once, when her mother was away on location, her former stepfather had a party. Rachel said there were a lot of drugs around.

I don't know anything about drugs or what

kind these were. All I know is that Rachel explained how those people acted on drugs and that's enough for me to tell you not to do them.

These people acted stupid, idiotic, foolish, moronic, asinine, imbecilic, fatuous—I looked up the word *dumb* in the thesaurus and found these other words.

The people on drugs couldn't walk or talk properly; they couldn't drive; they couldn't hold a drink without spilling it everywhere.

Does that not sound like being a baby? Have we not grown for these past twelve years just to get away from being babies? Do we really want to take pills or chemicals or whatever just so we can feel like infants? I don't.

I don't want to put myself in that kind of danger. And drugs are dangerous. They make you think you can do things you simply cannot do.

I know, I know. There is a curious bone in all our bodies. Also, some unfortunate kids think drugs are cool.

Let's think about a famous basketball player who died while using drugs. He was young and he was healthy. And he was a basketball player! And he was famous! But now he's dead, because

of drugs. Drugs didn't make him a good basketball player—they only killed him. End of game,
buzzer sounds, no halftime here. It's over.

If it could happen to him, it could happen
to you.

Don't make that same mistake.

24

don't smoke

there are several reasons why you should not smoke. Let's not forget that it's illegal to buy cigarettes if you're under eighteen.

If you smoke, you can kiss track and field goodbye. Your lungs are going to be filled with black junk, so you're not going to be able to run anywhere.

Come to think of it, if you smoke, you can kiss kissing goodbye, unless you date another smoker. Who wants to kiss an ashtray?

Another important reason not to smoke is that people who do certain things attract people who do similar things.

Now, I'm not meaning to judge, but most of

89

the people in my school, or at Beverly Hills Elementary, don't smoke.

The kids who smoke hang out with each other. To be blunt, these kids are *not* popular. They're rebels. Have you noticed that rebels are not popular?

Rebels might be unique and they might be fun to look at, but they spend most of their time doing things they're not supposed to do. That's why they're called rebellious. They usually get into a lot of trouble.

But do you want to know the number one reason why you shouldn't smoke? It's a beauty reason.

When you smoke, you age prematurely. Now, I'm not trying to scare you—you're not going to look like Grandma overnight. Slowly, however, your skin is going to grow tough, and it will wrinkle and your pores will get really big.

Rough skin and big pores are not attractive, and many women in Beverly Hills spend thousands of dollars to undo the damage smoking causes, by having painful plastic surgery.

Fun, huh?

25

be adventurous

don't confuse a dangerous situation with an adventurous one. A dangerous situation generally involves doing something that you know is not right or that would get you into trouble if your parents found out you were doing it.

For instance, shoplifting is dangerous.

Thrift shopping is adventurous.

Another example of danger: going into a deserted house. That's called trespassing, and it's illegal, by the way.

You want to know another example of being adventurous? Going up to a woman who works at the perfume counter and asking for a sample of perfume. (Ask for CK One.) It's fun, really, and it's a free way to get new perfume.

Dangerous: skipping school with a friend.

Adventurous: going to a play with a friend. (Your mom or dad might have to drive you, but it's well worth it. Plays are fun!)

Basically, a dangerous situation doesn't require much thought. All you have to do is follow someone else's lead into a situation that you know is not good for you.

Being adventurous is a little bit harder. It means being creative. You have to think of new things to do.

It's harder to be adventurous in Peoria than it is in Beverly Hills. There aren't as many cool things to do in Peoria as there were in sunny Southern California. So my best friend, Jackie, and I have to be very creative.

Every Saturday we write down five new, fun things to do. Then we put the ideas in a bowl and pick one.

We went to a museum one day. One Saturday we practically spent the whole day at the arcade. Or we've gone to the movies. Shopping is always a good alternative, of course.

One day we went to a bookstore and stayed

there all day! We read books on astrology and Europe and all these other crazy things. *That* was about our most adventurous outing yet. It rocked.

Anyway, being adventurous makes you feel older, more adult. Trust me and do it! You'll like it!!!

26

be kind to teachers

i don't believe that all adults are necessarily worthy of my respect. I know I'll probably get a lot of letters about this (particularly if your mother happens to read this), but I have met eight-year-olds who are worthy of more respect than certain forty-year-olds. Just because they're older doesn't mean they're wiser.

But we need to be nice to teachers because they have a hard job and don't get paid a lot of money. And they're educated at colleges. While an education doesn't necessarily make anyone worthy of respect, the fact that they know more about the world than you does.

I have to admit, I don't think following this rule will make you any more popular, at least not with the students. But it *will* make you more popular with the teachers. Who fills out your report cards?! 'Nough said. ☺

27

keep a journal

you might be wondering what this rule has to do with being popular, but it's very important, really. The better you know yourself, the better other people will be able to know you.

Writing about yourself is like leaving pieces of bread in a forest, like Hansel and Gretel. Remember them? Imagine that the things you write are like pieces of bread, and your life is like a forest. The trail of bread leads you through the forest so you don't get lost!

Your life can get pretty confusing at times, right? Well, it's pretty cool looking back at what you wrote a year ago. You'll see how much you've grown. Do you think I could have written this book without a journal?

As a matter of fact, my journal is going to be invaluable to me when I sit down to write a movie based on this book. In the movie, I'm going to go into more detail about me, my friends, and my family—things we've said or done, or maybe some of the funny things that have happened to us.

Keeping a journal is also an emotional release. You don't bottle things up when you write them down.

Madonna once had a hit song called "Express Yourself," and that's exactly what the journal is for: to make your thoughts and feelings known to nobody but yourself. This is your private little space that no one else can ever see.

Again, the best reason for writing the journal is that you get to know yourself better.

You might think you know yourself pretty well, but you'd be amazed at the things you can be holding in without even realizing it. Good and bad things.

For instance, a good thing you might be holding in is a natural talent for writing poetry. You could be a great poet and not even know it!

Poetry isn't like schoolwork. In poems, and in the journal, you can write about anything you want.

The journal can also show you some bad things that you might be hiding from yourself.

For instance, say a certain person keeps popping up in your journal. Maybe it's your sister, or possibly a good friend. Maybe you keep writing weird things about her, like she really bothered you today, or she makes you mad even when she doesn't say anything particularly hurtful or mean.

After a while, writing about this person will either help you let the bad feelings about them go, or you'll notice that you have an issue with them. Maybe your journal is helping you understand that you need to clear the air with this person.

Maybe you resent them for something you weren't even aware of. It's okay! Once you see the pattern, write more about the person and uncover what it is you *really* feel about them. You know why? Because when you recognize a problem, you can correct it.

So journals can help you find the good and bad things within you that need to be expressed.

The good things make you feel better about yourself, and writing the bad things helps you find an understanding of them.

All this leads back to a simple, happy fact: The better you *know* yourself, the happier you'll *feel* about yourself.

Now I'm starting to sound like a parrot, but it's the root of popularity.

A word of caution: There are some nosy people out there. You should keep your journal in a safe hiding place.

I had a friend in Beverly Hills named Stacey who kept a very personal journal. Her step-mother found the journal and read the entire thing! Can you believe it?! Stacey was so mad and hurt that she stopped writing in her journal. She really felt betrayed.

It burned me that Stacey's stepmother was cruel enough to read something that personal. And I knew how important it was for Stacey to write in her journal. But Stacey didn't feel comfortable writing anything personal anymore. So for Stacey's eleventh birthday, I bought her a nice leather journal with a *huge* lock on it!

It's funny. I could picture Stacey's step-mother working on that lock with a paper clip, desperate to know the secrets of her eleven-year-old stepdaughter. Get a life, lady! Anyhow, it doesn't matter. The lock was very sturdy, and now Stacey keeps her journal in her bag at all times.

My point is, if you feel for any reason that someone might snoop in your journal when you aren't around, get a journal with a lock and keep it in a special hiding place. But keep a journal!

say "thank you" once a day

Okay, you're ready to cart me off to the school nurse. How the heck is saying "Thank you" going to make me popular? you're probably asking yourself. Well, I'll tell you how.

The words "Thank you" imply that you're satisfied with something. And there are probably a dozen things that happen in your day to make you feel happy and satisfied. But if you don't feel it's important to say "Thank you," you might start taking all the good things that happen for granted.

For instance, every day my mother makes me lunch. I used to think she was being mean because most of the other kids get to buy their

101

lunches. But then I started looking at what the other kids were eating. Gross! My leftovers are usually better than what they serve at school.

I mean, I saw a piece of meat in the cafeteria that was iridescent! (*Iridescent* means "having a rainbow play of color." I only know the word because I bought a jacket at a thrift store and the man said it was iridescent. He explained to me what it meant!) Anyway, every day I see my mom making my lunch and I know she could be sleeping in. It means a lot to me that she takes the time to get up and make my lunch. I always tell her, "Thank you."

Then there are the bus drivers. Okay, maybe they're paid to drive us to school, but it's not a very fun job. My bus driver is way over thirty, and I'm sure he would rather be doing something else than driving the dumb bus. Maybe he likes it, I don't know. But every day when I get off the bus, I say, "Thank you." He always says, "You're welcome." I feel good when he says that.

Saying "Thank you" is about the easiest thing you can do during the day. It doesn't cost anything and it doesn't take any effort. No one is going to laugh at you when you say it, and it's another way to make sure you're being a nice person.

When someone gives an adult a present, the person who receives the present usually sends a thank-you card. I'm sure your mom and dad have done it, and they do it because it's common courtesy.

If you don't believe me that saying "Thank you" can make you popular, ask your mom or dad what would happen if they received a gift but didn't send a thank-you card.

They might tell you this: "If I didn't send a thank-you card for a gift, the person giving me the gift might think I was rude."

And if you asked, "What would happen if they thought you were rude?" your parents would probably say, "They might not give me a gift the next time around."

Popularity is a gift. Saying "Thank you" is a way of appreciating that gift.

And what's the one thing I've told you from the start? If you're nice, you feel better about yourself. If you feel better about yourself, *other* people will feel better about you!

don't be confused or frightened by the upcoming changes

this is me getting serious: ☺

I must admit this is another rule my mom encouraged me to write. And I have to admit that I'm writing this mostly with the help of my mom, and Sara, and the research I have done. Because, you see, well . . . I haven't gone through it yet. The big P. *Puberty.* In fact, before my mom and Sara started talking about it, I really didn't even know what "it" was.

"It" is this thing our bodies are about to go through. The big change-a-roo. Supposedly, most girls go through it around age twelve and a half. For some it's sooner; for others it's later.

My sister, Sara, said the change made her more aware of herself. She said I would know more about what she was saying when I started going through it myself.

Sara said I could ask her questions about what I would soon be going through, which I am sure she did not need to encourage me to do. I ask a million questions about little things; I'm sure to ask a lot of questions about *that*!

I encourage all my readers to research puberty for themselves. I also encourage you to talk with your parents, sisters, or counselors, if need be, about the upcoming changes.

When puberty hits, there will be a lot of changes. We will change physically, emotionally, and mentally. All these changes are good. Our sisters and our brothers went through them. Our parents went through them.

Every person goes through puberty as they mature. It's a wacky part of maturing. But again, the process of maturing brings with it a lot of questions. Use a lot of the rules listed above. Talk, ask questions, etc.

One of the best things I've read about puberty is that the way we *think* will change.

According to a famous psychologist who has researched this change, puberty brings with it the chance for us kids to think in deeper ways.

That sounds exciting to me. Who knows? Maybe I'm going through puberty already. Maybe that's why I am writing this book! ☺

When *your* puberty comes, I hope the transition is a happy and fun one!!

30

the final rule!!!!

In conclusion, I want to say one last thing: The best way for people to feel good about you is for *you* to feel good about yourself.

Okay, okay, I know I've said this before, but really it's the root of this book. All the rules in one way or another have something to do with helping you feel good about yourself.

Popularity is not a goal, it's an adventure! It's fun finding out who you are because then you can share the good qualities with other people. It's that happy circle again, like the smiley face! ☺

But I want you to remember something: Sometimes when we have nice things, or wear good clothes, people like us for those things. But sometimes we do *not* have nice things or wear good clothes, and maybe people do *not* pay attention to us. But that's okay!

If your sixth-grade year is not going very well, you have to look at it this way: Sixth grade is usually only nine months, minus vacations and weekends. Really only 180 days. Then there's seventh grade, and you have a whole year to like yourself even better. And the more you like yourself, the less important it's going to be for other people to like you. In a way, that *might* make them like you more.

But I'm telling you, and you have to trust me on this, being popular is not *the* most important thing in your life. How you *feel* about yourself is *the* most important thing. So, my last and most important rule is:

BE NICE TO *YOURSELF*!

2 part
two

q: How do I kiss?

a: My first question is: Do you really want to? J.k.

Okay, call me terminally unhip (translation: a goody-goody), but I am still at the hand-holding stage, so in terms of kissing I can only offer my clinical viewpoint.

First you need to touch lips. I think worldwide this is the most accepted form of kissing. We're not Eskimos or else we might rub noses, though they probably only do that so their lips don't freeze together.

I hope you don't wear braces, because then kissing could get ugly and painful. You might want to talk to your orthodontist about this how-to-kiss situation.

In terms of French kissing (you know, that loud and somewhat disgusting exchange of food particles and saliva?), I think this is definitely better left to experience at a later date when you don't have to write a question regarding how to kiss.

Who knows, if you attempt French kissing right away, you might end up drowning in your partner's saliva!

q: How do I make a boy like me?

a: First, send me your name and address and I'll send you a copy of my book. Because from my book you will hopefully get the following message: The most important thing to do to make someone like you is to like yourself.

Have you ever seen that movie *Mommie Dearest*? If you haven't, I command you to *go rent it now*! J.k., inside joke.

Mommie Dearest is about a very mean woman who hated wire hangers and used force and manipulation to make people notice her. She was not very nice, and I don't think there is any nice way to *make* somebody like you.

If you like a boy who doesn't appear to show any interest in you, don't force yourself on him. Don't try to compete with the girl(s) he seems to like. Simply be yourself. Follow the above rules. Develop your own style. Talk. Smile as much as humanly possible without looking like a raving madgirl.

If he still doesn't like you, be okay with that. Trust me, there is a boy out there who is going to like you. It might even be this boy you like. It might not be this year, but maybe next. Or the year after. Boys are very unpredictable.

I think my next book will be called *How to Figure Out Boys in the Sixth Grade*. But there's probably not enough paper in the world for that book!

q: I like this guy, but he's dating another girl I do not like. How can I break them up?

a: You can't. You know why? Because you're not supposed to. No one came down and handed you a magic wand and said, "Here, you. Break this couple up!" Until that happens, leave them alone.

Couples, like pimples, should go away naturally. If you force them to go away, you'll end up causing scars. And who knows—maybe *you* will be the one scarred.

q: I'm not very popular right now, but I want to be. If I follow your rules, will it really make me popular?

a: I could not put a 1000% guarantee on the cover of this book because nothing is ever 1000% guaranteed. Popularity is a very hard thing to judge. How do you ever really know if you're popular?

Maybe you're already popular but you just don't see it. Do people like talking to you? Do you feel good about yourself?

At my new school, Peoria Middle School, there is a girl named Shannon who came from a small town in Maine. Shannon tells me that at her old school, their class had three tables reserved for them in the lunchroom.

The popular kids set the tables up as follows: A table, B table, and C table. The popular kids sat at the A table, the midlevel popular kids sat at the B table, and the less popular kids sat at the C table.

How stupid is that? I would have sat at the

C table in defiance of the A table people. I might be popular at my school now, but I say this only because people know who I am and they like talking to me. I also have to admit that I'm the biggest talker I know of, so *that* has a lot to do with my popularity.

If you have to determine your popularity by where you sit, or what you wear, or who your best friend is, then this is fleeting popularity. It will go away at some point.

Remember what I said earlier? The one thing no one can take away from you is the fact that you're a nice person. And if you're a nice person, people will like you. That's one of the most important aspects of popularity—people *like* you.

q: My dad is in the military and we're moving next year and I'm scared. What if I can't make any friends?

a: Offer them money. J.k. Seriously, it's okay to be nervous about the move. That's to be expected. But really, what you're being given here is the opportunity for a whole new beginning!

No one at this new school will know you. You've been given a brand-new start! And you know what? If you follow each and every one of my rules, you'll have no problem making friends. You probably won't have any problem making friends anyway, but these rules will help.

I kind of know what you're going through— the anxiety, I mean. I moved to three schools during my elementary years, but each time it got easier and easier to fit in. I guess you could say I had a lot of practice.

Since you're the daughter of a military man, I would imagine you've moved quite a bit. So you're probably an expert on making new friends and don't even know it yet. But don't you *dare* write a book about popularity or I'll sue you! J.k.

Seriously, I think you'll do fine. Write and let me know how things are going for you!

q: How do you get kids to stop picking on you?

a: This is a very serious question, so I'm not going to crack any jokes. If kids pick on you, I think this is a very bad situation and one that makes me feel really sad.

I mentioned earlier in my book how a group of us kids used to pick on Becky because she was from Texas. It just makes me so guilty to think about it.

Kids of America, I want you to quit picking on other kids this very second! It's not right and it's not fair, and someday you too are going to feel very guilty about it.

If you're being picked on by another person, the first thing to remember is that it's not your fault. You are *not* the one with the problem.

The person picking on you is doing it because they feel insecure about themselves! They need to pick on other people to feel better about themselves. In a way, they feel hurt— they're simply taking that hurt out on you.

If anyone ever, *ever* tries to push or hit you, I want you to go immediately to an adult you trust and tell that adult what's happened. This is a matter for an adult to handle. I abhor physical violence and believe it's best not to sink to that level. An adult will be able to make sure this person is dealt with appropriately. In fact, whenever someone picks on you in any way, it's best to seek advice from an adult you trust.

From my own personal experience I've learned that the only way for words to hurt you is if you let them. You know that saying—sticks and stones can break my bones but words will never hurt me? We learned that in, like, kindergarten, but it still holds true.

Don't give another person the power over you to hurt your feelings. If someone is making fun of your name, or your clothes, or even your accent, tell them, "You're the one with the problem," and leave it at that. Because that person *is* the one with the problem.

Insecure people pick on other people. If anyone picks on you, they're insecure. There's nothing wrong with *you*.

Best of luck, and I feel for you.

q: How important is it to be popular?

a: Believe it or not, it *is* important. Before I started writing this book, I did some research. According to my investigation, up until we're twelve, "fitting in" is *the* most important thing for us. We're popularity *mongers* or something. I guess at this age popularity is our main dream and our goal.

Not only is it *important* to us, but popularity is also *good* for us. You see, when we feel liked by others, we tend to do better in school and in other social situations. As always, though, the most important thing is for us to feel good about *ourselves*.

Even if we're popular in the old-fashioned sense—like we sit at the A table or something stupid like that—if we don't feel good about ourselves, it doesn't matter who likes us or not. Unless we're happy with ourselves, popularity is meaningless.

I hope that if you learn anything from my book, it's that you, me, and everyone else are very special people. We should love each other, and we should love ourselves.

q: A lot of girls in my class are start-ing to wear makeup. My mom says I can't wear it until I get to high school. All the other girls think I'm an alien from another galaxy because I can't even wear lipstick. Should I just put makeup on once I get to school, then wipe it off before I get home? Help!

a: My advice is to stay away from makeup until you know how to use it. Otherwise, you really *will* look like an alien from another galaxy.

I'm sure you've seen the unfortunate attempts some girls make when they first start using makeup?

First of all, they have no idea what colors look good on them. They usually just copy the makeup used on a model in a magazine, without any clue (hence the term *clueless*) that hair and skin color plays a very important role in the type and shades of makeup they should be using.

Secondly, I am not real keen on your idea of wearing makeup despite your mother telling you not to. What happens if you forget to wipe something off? What if you get lipstick on your shirt? It's inevitable that one day you'll miss something, and your mom is sure to catch on. Do you want to risk getting in trouble?

Also, you don't want to borrow someone else's makeup, because you can get germs. (Don't laugh, it's true. My friend Brie in fifth grade got pink-eye because she borrowed her sixth-grade friend's mascara!)

You don't want to steal makeup, because at the very least you will get grounded.

The final reason I think you should wait to wear makeup is because I am what you call a nature lover—I think the natural look is the way to go.

When we get into high school there's going to be plenty of time for us to experiment with makeup and different hair colors. We'll be able to get jobs. That way we can afford to look really *FIERCE*!

q: Why are you writing this dumb girly book?!

a: These questions were supposed to be from girls, but obviously *this* one wasn't. This was obviously written by some Neanderthal boy—like he could fool me with *that* question.

final words

sniffle...
sniffle.

☹

This is so long for now—but not goodbye forever!!!!

I hope you had as much fun reading this book as I had writing it! I also hope you get some use out of my rules on *How to Be Popular in the Sixth Grade*.

As you can imagine, these rules aren't *only* for sixth-graders. They're for fourth- and fifth-grade girls, too. If you work on these rules, regardless of what grade you're in, you're going to be *way* ahead of the pack in terms of making friends and fitting in and all that good stuff.

So I guess my point is—tell others about the book! Share the wealth, as I like to say. Lend them my book if you want. Have parties and talk about my rules! Send me questions, success stories, etc. I've left my Web site address at the back of this book, so I'd better hear from you!!

Bye, everyone!!!

Peace and love,
Camy Baker

reference

reference

rules at a glance

for easy reference

1. Forget the rules.

2. Don't follow trends—set them!

3. Be the nicest person in your class.

4. Talk, talk, talk.

5. Learn one new word a week.

6. Be charming.

7. Seek advice.

8. Don't bottle it up.

9. Choose your mirrors carefully.

10. Be independent.

11. Ask questions.

12. You don't know it all,

so don't pretend to.

13. Be humble.

14. Be the smartest person in your class.

15. Stand tall.

16. Be yourself.

17. Develop a talent.

18. Be by yourself—it's okay.

19. Find a friend.

20. Don't cling to friends, boyfriends,

or popularity.

21. Don't be jealous of anybody.

22. Laugh and smile as much as

humanly possible.

23. Don't do drugs.

24. Don't smoke.

25. Be adventurous.

26. Be kind to teachers.

27. Keep a journal.

28. Say "Thank you" once a day.

29. Don't be confused or frightened by the upcoming changes.

30. BE NICE TO YOURSELF!!!!

cool words to learn

....

....

....

....

....

....

....

....

....

....

....

....

....

cool words to learn

and finally, check out

web site
www.camybaker.com

see ya there!!!

bye!

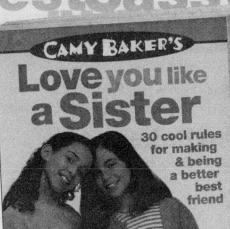